Copyright © 2017 MARVEL

# Lending a Wing

Written by Arie Kaplan

Illustrated by Ron Lim and Rachelle Rosenberg

Based on the Marvel comic book series The Avengers

Los Angeles • New York

Usually, people noticed Sam Wilson, especially when he was Falcon. But that day Sam hoped that wouldn't happen. He had gone undercover to expose a crime ring. He was pretending to be one of the bad guys to catch them in the act. He made sure to dress the part so he didn't stand out. He didn't want anyone to suspect that he was secretly an Avenger!

When Sam left to meet the crooks, his pet falcon, Redwing, followed him. At the meeting, Redwing circled Sam.

A burly blond thief named Hoyt pointed at Sam's feathered friend and yelled, "Hey, that's Redwing, Falcon's pet bird!" He stared hard at Sam. "That means *you're* Falcon!" he cried.

*So much for flying under the radar,* Sam thought. He put his hands up, ready for a fight.

Hoyt and the other crooks had Sam and Redwing surrounded.

"Looks like we caged the Falcon, boys," Hoyt growled to his friends.

With Redwing's help, Sam fought his way out of the den of thieves. The duo was severely outnumbered, but they were trained for these kinds of tough situations, even without Sam's Falcon suit.

Sam and Redwing led the crooks on a lengthy chase. Soon they found themselves cornered in an alley. Hoyt and his men were getting tired, but Sam had saved his strength. He was sure the fight was about to go his way.

Hoyt glared at Sam. "What are you gonna do now, fly away?" he jeered.

Before Sam could say anything, he saw a flash of red, white, and blue. Suddenly, Captain America appeared in front of him.

Cap sized up the situation. Then, without a moment's hesitation, he landed a strong right hook on Hoyt's jaw.

Sam and Redwing followed Cap's lead, attacking the thieves. The heroes quickly defeated the criminals.

With Cap's help, Sam and Redwing captured the thieves and turned them over to the police.

Later, at Avengers Tower, Falcon was distracted. He tried to clear his head by practicing his moves on the punching bag in the gym.

Captain America watched from the doorway. "Good team-up earlier," he said. But Falcon just kept punching the bag.

Cap walked over and put a hand on Falcon's shoulder. Falcon tried to smile, but he just didn't have it in him. Finally, he said, "I didn't need your help. I was doing fine on my own."

Then he turned and stomped away, leaving Cap stunned.

Falcon needed to clear his head. With a running start, he took to the air over New York. The feeling of the wind beneath his wings relaxed him.

As he soared high above the clouds, Falcon muttered, "Real heroes don't need to be rescued."

Just thinking about needing help made him angry. It made him feel *weak*.

But the longer he flew, the more Falcon realized he shouldn't have been so rude to Cap. It wasn't Captain America's fault that Falcon had needed help. He was just being a good friend.

Just then, Falcon glanced at a rooftop below and spotted Black Widow. She was waving to him.

Falcon flew down to see what Black Widow needed. The spy explained that Captain America was in trouble. He needed their help.

Sam couldn't believe his ears. "Why would *Cap* need help?" he said.

"Everyone needs a helping hand from time to time," said Black Widow. "Even a Super-Soldier."

Falcon knew Black Widow was right. Following her directions, he flew off to find his friend.

He quickly reached the location Black Widow had given him. But Cap was nowhere to be found. Falcon perched on a branch and looked around.

Finally, Falcon spied Cap. He was on a nearby rooftop . . . surrounded by Hydra agents! Captain America was using his shield to fight them off, but he was outnumbered.

Falcon lowered himself to a neighboring roof and looked around for Black Widow. Captain America needed their help . . . now!

Falcon saw Black Widow on the next rooftop and gestured to her.

Black Widow nodded in reply. Then, leaping into action, she shot a string of blasts at the unsuspecting Hydra agents.

Black Widow kept the Hydra goons so distracted with her fast and furious fighting style that they didn't even see Falcon flying toward them.

Falcon had nearly reached Cap when a Hydra agent strapped on a jet pack and took off—with Cap in his evil clutches.

Falcon flew after him. He chased the airborne Hydra spy tirelessly, zigzagging through the air. Finally, Falcon caught up to the spy. He knocked out the green-clad thug with a thundering *THWACK!*

Falcon realized that the unconscious villain had let go of Cap, who was now plummeting helplessly toward the roof below. With seconds to spare, Sam swooped down and caught his friend by the arm!

Falcon lowered the powerful patriot toward the roof just in time for Cap to hurl his shield at a horde of Hydra operatives.

The Hydra agents fell to the ground like a row of bowling pins. It was truly a *strike* against Hydra!

Working together, Falcon, Black Widow, and Captain America quickly defeated the remaining Hydra agents. The Avengers captured the enemy spies, proving that Earth's Mightiest Heroes were even more heroic as a team.

Later, back at Avengers Tower, Iron Man shook Falcon's hand. "Good job today," he said. "The Avengers could use a guy like you around!"

Falcon smiled. "You know," he said. "I learned a tough lesson today. Real bravery is admitting when you need help . . . and apologizing when you're wrong."

Falcon turned to Cap. "I'm sorry about the way I acted earlier," he said. "If you hadn't given me a hand back in that alley—"

"Don't sweat it," Cap said, cutting him off.

Falcon knew now that his friends had his back, and he had theirs. And that made him feel like the luckiest person in the world!